TWO...

by CHARLOTTE ZOLOTOW

illustrated by
ROGER DUVOISIN

LOTHROP, LEE & SHEPARD COMPANY
NEW YORK

ONE STEP

Library of Congress Catalog Card Number: 55-7027

9 10 75 74 73 72

12 steps

For Ellen
who showed me
many mornings.

One spring morning, the mother and her little girl came down the steps of their house—one step, two steps, three steps—and they were down. They started to walk to the corner.

"See that!" said the little girl.

"What?" asked the mother.

And then she saw—a little yellow crocus shining in the grass.

One Step, two steps, three steps more.

"Come," said the mother.

But the little girl stood still. "Look!" she said.

The mother looked, and then she saw it, too—a little grey cat prowling through the bushes next door.

One step, two steps, three steps, four—and the little girl stopped again.

"See *that!*" she said, and pointed to a bluebird floating down to earth with its white-tipped wings spread wide.

One step, two . . . three, four, five steps—and six. The little girl stooped down, and picked up a round white pebble that gleamed in the sun like a little pale moon.

One, two, three, four, five, six, seven steps.

"See!" said the little girl.

And her mother saw the dresses and pants and towels dancing on the line.

One, two, three, four, five, six, seven, eight, nine steps.

"Clip clip clippety clop, clop clop clippety clip

"Hear that!" said the little girl.

It was the milkman's horse passing on the other side of the street.

BUTTER
EGGS

One, two, three, four, five, six, seven, eight, nine, ten, eleven . . .

Suddenly the bells of the church burst into music like a flock of birds in the sky. The little girl took her mother's hand and stood still and listened until
they stopped ringing.

Then she went on.

One, two, three, four, five, six, seven, eight, nine, ten, eleven, and twelve . . .

They had reached the end of the block.

"Truck," the little girl said as the school bus whished by.

"Lunchtime," said the mother. She took her little girl's hand and they started home.

SCHOOL
BUS
NO
PARKING
BUS
STOP

One, two, three, four, five, six steps toward home. The little girl bent down to pick some daffodils swelling yellow on their flat stems.

"Oh no," said her mother, "they are not ours! But you may smell them."

Sniff, sniff, sniff! The little girl wrinkled her nose.

One, two, three, four, five, six, seven . . .

The little girl stopped and her eyes grew round. There right in front of them was a hurdy-gurdy man with a furry little monkey perched on his hand.

"How do, little girl," said the hurdy-gurdy man.

But she had no words for him at all. She was too surprised.

One, two, three, four, five, six, seven, eight, nine, ten—

They passed a house with plants in the window.

"Pretty!" said the little girl.

"Yes," agreed her mother. "Red geraniums!"

One, two, three, four, five, six, seven, eight, nine, ten, e-l-e-v-e-n, t-w-e-l-v-e . . .

"Home again!" said the mother as they turned up the walk to their house.

But at the stairs, the little girl turned around.

"Up," she said, reaching with both arms.

Her mother gathered her up and hugged her close.

"What a lovely walk, and what a lot of things we saw. Thank you little girl for showing me—

The hurdy-gurdy man,
The yellow daffodils,
The clothes drying in the sun,
The milkman's horse clopping by,
The blue jay flying in the sky,
The little crocus,
The prowling cat,
The small white pebble like a moon,
The lovely bells that rang at noon."

But the little girl didn't hear. She was fast asleep.